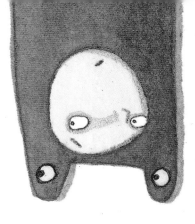

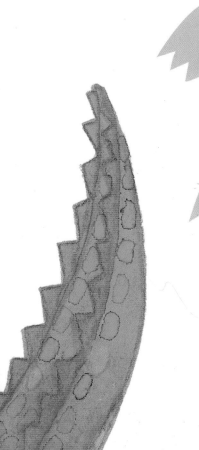

WANTED!
Have You Seen This
ALligator?

WANTED! Have

For Fern and Sofia – R.W.

For Matt and my family,
all my love and thanks x – H.S.

First published in 2002 in Great Britain by

GULLANE
CHILDREN'S BOOKS

Winchester House, 259-269 Old Marylebone Road,
London NW1 5XJ

3 5 7 9 10 8 6 4 2

Text © Richard Waring 2002
Illustrations © Holly Swain 2002

The right of Richard Waring and Holly Swain to be identified as the author and illustrator of this work
has been asserted by them in accordance with the Copyright, Designs, and Patents Act, 1988.
A CIP record for this title is available from the British Library.

ISBN 1-86233-386-6 hardback
ISBN 1-86233-462-5 paperback

Printed and bound in Belgium

You Seen This Alligator?

Richard Waring ≈ Holly Swain

GULLANE
CHILDREN'S BOOKS

Tina was given a rather large and peculiar-looking egg by her Uncle Ezra. She wrapped it in a soft blanket and put it on her bedside table.

That night, Tina heard a strange tapping
sound coming from the egg.
The shell began to crack and a little snout
pushed its way out. Then two eyes appeared
and stared at her!
Tina gasped.

It was a baby
alligator!

Tina called the alligator
Alberto – Alberto Alligator.
She loved Alberto and
Alberto loved her.
Very soon he grew into
a big alligator and so
Tina kept him in the bath.

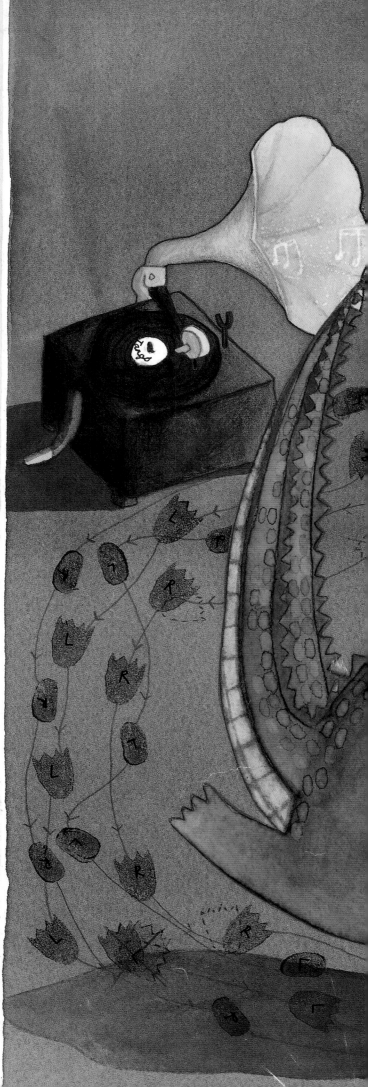

He loved music, particularly the tango, and they would dance together for hours to the sound of his favourite record . . .

. . . although he could never get the footing quite right.

Then, one day, a terrible thing happened.
Whilst dancing in the bathroom, Tina and
Alberto **slipped** on a bar of soap.

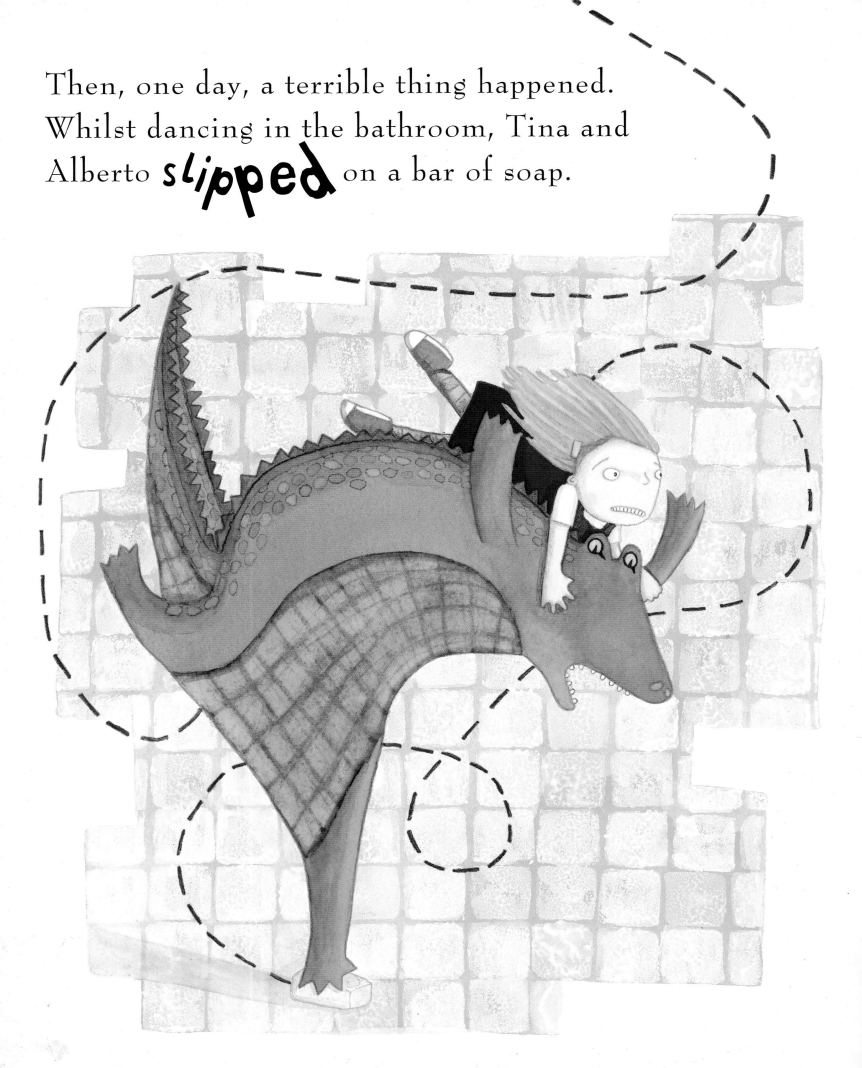

Alberto fell head first into the toilet!
As Tina fell, she grabbed the toilet flusher,
and **WHOOSH** . . .

. . . Alberto was **gone!**

Down, down, down went Alberto,
to the world way below the city.
Alberto thought it was
a great adventure.

He slid along pipes . . .

. . . and splashed in large pools . .

... he played and swam ...

... and swam and played.

Then, when he was tired, he decided it was time to go home.

Alberto climbed up one of the tall pipes until he reached a bathroom. But it was the wrong one! An old lady saw him,

screamed

and called the police.

eeeeek

there's an alligator in my toilet!

Alberto climbed up the next pipe along, leading to the next apartment. The plumber saw him,

screamed

and also called the police.

...green...
...about 25 teeth...

Alberto went from bathroom to bathroom . . .

. . . and each time someone saw him, they screamed and

alled the police. That day, dozens of different people . . .

. . . called dozens of different police officers
to report an alligator in their bathroom.

Very quickly, the rumour spread.
The newspaper reported:

**1000 ALLIGATORS
ON THE LOOSE,
ALL BATHROOMS
AT RISK!**

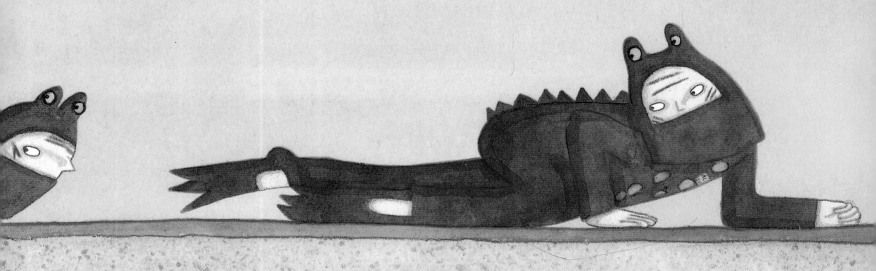

called the army, and the army called the experts.

Expert alligator hunters,
trained to hunt alligators,
went down into the deep,
dark, murky tunnels of the city's sewers.

The whole city was at a standstill. Everyone waited for the first alligator to be caught. Television and radio gave a moment by moment account of the search party's progress.

Tina and her dad saw the news.
They were both very worried for Alberto.
Tina ran to the bathroom and tried
calling Alberto's name loudly
down the toilet, but to no avail.

Then Tina had a better idea . . .

Down in the sewers, Alberto could
hear the splish, splash, swish
of the alligator hunters.
He could see their shadows.
He was scared.
The hunters were getting closer
and closer to their target —
not one thousand alligators,
not even one hundred alligators . . .

. . . but one small, friendly but frightened Alberto.

Suddenly, a strange sound echoed through the tunnels . . .

. . . it was the music of the tango!
If an alligator could smile, he did.
It was Tina! She was playing his favourite record.

Alberto followed the sound as fast as he could . . .

Alberto climbed
back into his
own bathroom.
Back to Tina.
He was safe at last.

Alberto hugged
Tina and Tina
hugged Alberto.

GIANT
PIGEON
EXPERTS
CALLED IN

When the search party
found nothing,
they gave up, and
the city soon forgot
all about alligators.

Alberto!

Tina took Alberto
to the animal sanctuary where
he now lives with the other alligators.
Though he comes home every weekend . . .

. . . so they can practise their tango steps together.